WELCOME TO

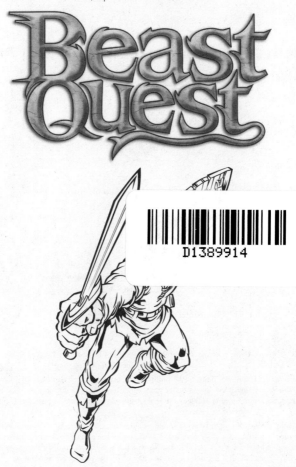

Beast Quest

Collect the special coins in this book.
You will earn one gold coin for
every chapter you read.

Once you have finished all the chapters,
find out what to do with your gold coins at
the back of the book.

With special thanks to Allan Frewin Jones

For Lewis Coleman

www.beastquest.co.uk

ORCHARD BOOKS

First published in Great Britain in 2014 by The Watts Publishing Group
This edition published in 2018 by The Watts Publishing Group

1 3 5 7 9 10 8 6 4 2

Text © 2014 Beast Quest Limited.
Cover and inside illustrations by Steve Sims
© Beast Quest Limited 2014

Beast Quest is a registered trademark of Beast Quest Limited
Series created by Beast Quest Limited, London

A CIP catalogue record for this book is available from the British Library.

ISBN 978 1 40835 869 6

Printed and bound in Germany

The paper and board used in this book are made from wood from responsible sources

Orchard Books
An imprint of Hachette Children's Group
Part of The Watts Publishing Group Limited
Carmelite House, 50 Victoria Embankment, London EC4Y 0DZ

An Hachette UK Company
www.hachette.co.uk
www.hachettechildrens.co.uk

TIKRON
THE JUNGLE MASTER

BY ADAM BLADE

ORCHARD

CONTENTS

Dear reader,

Do not pity me – my spells may be useless now, but my sixth sense will never go. Evil is afoot in this once peaceful kingdom. Jezrin the Judge may have been defeated by brave Tom, but his minions do not rest. Our many Quests have taught me that an enemy beaten back will return stronger than before.

Tonight I had a vision of the pale moon turning black. What it means is not clear, but a new menace stalks the land of Rion, and I fear it will spread to Avantia. My wizard instincts tell me that our enemies plan to tip the balance of nature, turning Good to Evil. A hero will be needed to stand against the dark forces. Can you guess who that hero might be?

Aduro, former wizard to King Hugo

PROLOGUE

Polk whooped and cheered as he swung through the jungle trees. He made his way from branch to branch, snatching at dangling nuts and clusters of fruit, and throwing them skilfully into the woven sack looped over his shoulders.

His sister's voice rang out. "Be careful, Polk! You're too far away from the others."

Laughing, he ignored her warning call. It would be the Feast of the Full Moon soon, and this was the first time the tribe had allowed him to go foraging for food on his own.

"I know what I'm doing," he muttered to himself, as he snatched at a dangling vine and launched himself towards the next tree.

"The jungle is dangerous!" Imma shouted. "Don't be foolish!"

"I'll be fine!" Polk called back. But as he swung, his hands slipped on the vine and he plummeted. He clawed frantically at the approaching branches, only just managing to get a foothold.

His heart beating hard, he clung to the tree, gasping for breath. *That was too close!* The ground was a long way beneath him. If he had fallen, he would have broken bones for sure.

As his panic faded, he grinned again. "Ha!" This was a toko tree – and he could see the juicy, plump purple fruit hanging high up on the top branches.

He climbed up, then wedged himself between the branch and the trunk, taking his flint knife from his belt. But as he reached for the delicious fruit, a tremendous roar echoed through the jungle. The noise shook the branches and it was all Polk could do to hang on.

He heard the terrified voices of the other foragers. "Lion!"

Trembling, Polk peered down

through the trees. Was it really a lion? The great tawny creatures didn't usually come this far into the jungle.

"Polk!" Imma shouted. "Come back! We must go."

"I'm coming!" Polk cried, turning and making his way back towards the safety of the tribe.

Polk glanced over his shoulder as a second roar shook the jungle. The sound had come not from the ground below him, but from high in the leafy branches above.

He hurled himself through the air. Leaves parted and he saw his sister's anxious face staring at him, her eyes widening in horror. She was staring at something over his shoulder – something that utterly terrified her.

His heart pumping, Polk looked back once again.

Thick branches snapped like twigs as an enormous monkey surged into view. Polk had never seen such a monstrous creature. Its mouth was filled with vicious, dagger-sharp fangs. Its beady eyes glowed with anger and hatred. It had a wild, shaggy mane, and enormous muscles rippled beneath its dull brown fur.

As Polk stood, petrified with terror, the monkey-Beast roared again, spittle spraying from its gaping red mouth, the blast of its foul breath filling Polk's nostrils with a disgusting stench. The monkey's great pointed claws tore the branches aside, shaking the trees so that the

whole world seemed to heave and
sway under Polk's feet.

He saw spears cutting through the
air towards the Beast, and heard the
hiss of blow-darts. The tribe was
fighting back! But the spears glanced
off the monster's thick hide, and the

blow-darts snagged harmlessly in its shaggy fur.

A few brave warriors drew closer, shouting at the monster, brandishing their weapons. One tall, powerful man launched his spear at the monkey's eyes. But the Beast flung its arm up, batting the spear away before hurling itself from side to side, the trees swaying and bending as though in a hurricane.

"Flee for your lives!" cried one of the elders.

Everyone began to run, scattering back through the jungle. Polk turned to Imma. She was standing with her back to the tree trunk, frozen in horror.

"Sister, quickly!" he cried, grabbing her arm.

But they had hardly moved when Polk's head was filled with a hideous, high-pitched screech. He flung his hands up over his ears as Imma slid to her knees, grimacing in pain.

Polk tried to pull her onto her feet, but the Beast's deafening screech seemed to numb his limbs, turning his muscles to water and his bones to straw. He stumbled, disorientated, his head spinning.

He glanced back and saw the Beast's fangs dripping with saliva as its head came closer. A massive brown claw reached out to crush him.

RACE AGAINST TIME

The wind rushed in Tom's ears as Ferno flew onwards. The fire dragon's great leathery wings beat slowly and steadily, bearing Tom and Elenna and their two animal companions away from the Ruby Desert.

"I'm enjoying the cool air up here," Tom said to Elenna. "Fighting snakes in a baking hot desert was hard work."

Elenna glanced back towards the rolling sand dunes. "But the giant serpent Vislak is Good again now – Kensa's power over her has gone."

Tom nodded in grim satisfaction. *That battle is over, but the war is far from won.*

Kensa the Sorceress had returned to Avantia more deadly than ever, determined to seize control of the kingdoms. She had used a terrible spell to poison the six young Beasts of Rion, stealing their goodness. Only Vedra the green dragon had not yet come under her thrall – but he had been infected with Kensa's lunar blood potion, like the others. At that very moment, he lay in a chamber beneath King Hugo's palace. His green scales were slowly turning to black, and by the next full moon the transformation to Evil would be complete.

All that could save him was a medicine – the Gilded Elixir – made from four ingredients scattered in the corners of the kingdom. Each was guarded by a cursed Beast of Rion intent on killing Tom and Elenna.

Tom shuddered to think what would happen if Vedra fell under Kensa's spell.

Tom had already saved two of the Good Beasts and he had two of the elixir's ingredients in his pouch. But he knew Kensa would stop at nothing to prevent him claiming the remaining ones.

Tom glanced over his shoulder to check that his companions were all right. Storm was lying on Ferno's broad back, his legs folded up under him and the wind ruffling his mane. Silver the wolf lay at Elenna's side, his grey head in her lap, his yellow eyes bright.

Tom unrolled the magical map. "The next Beast, Tikron the Jungle Master, will be lurking in the Dark Jungle," he said aloud.

Elenna nodded slowly. She was sitting beside him, looking at the map. "There will be plenty of hiding places for him there," she muttered.

Tom agreed. "We'll keep watch for him while we search for the third ingredient," he said. "The red root from the hidden tree." He frowned as he peered at the map in the growing gloom of the evening. "But what's a 'hidden tree'? And how are we to find it in such a huge jungle?"

As Ferno flew on eastwards, night fell and ghostly clouds hung low in the sky.

"There's the Dark Jungle," Elenna said with a shudder, pointing to a wide, dark streak on the horizon.

Tom nodded. *What fresh peril could be lurking in that sinister place?*

"Go down, now, Ferno," he called.

The Beast spiralled downwards and landed on the east bank of the river. Tom and Elenna and their loyal animal companions jumped down from Ferno's back. "You have to go back now," Tom said to him. "I can't risk Kensa's spell turning you bad."

Ferno narrowed his eyes, as though he didn't want to leave his friends in danger, but then he nodded his massive head. With a flurry of wingbeats, he rose into the air and began his long flight home.

As they watched him go, a point of bright blue light ignited in the air just ahead of them. The light expanded, and the wizard, Daltec, appeared, his image shimmering.

"You were right to send Ferno away," Daltec told them. "You are doing well, but time is short." He pointed into the sky. A space appeared briefly in the scudding clouds and Tom could see that the moon was almost full.

Daltec made a pass with his hand and a vision of Vedra appeared. The young dragon lay unmoving in the great underground chamber, with Wilfred the Beast Keeper at his side.

"No!" gasped Tom in shock. Most of the green scales on the dragon's lithe body had turned black, as though he had been scorched by flames.

The vision disappeared and Daltec looked at them with worried eyes. "You have little time," he said, the blue light already fading. "Fare you well. Avantia's fate is in your hands."

The blue light winked out.

Tom turned to Elenna, his heart filled with renewed determination. "Kensa's spell must be destroyed," he said, gripping the hilt of his sword. "And whatever Evil awaits us, we will defeat it – or die in the attempt!"

INTO THE DARK

They headed towards the jungle,
Tom and Elenna mounted on Storm's
back, Silver prowling ahead, sniffing
for danger.

The sun was just rising as they
rode in under the trees. Shards of
light stabbed down through the
canopy of leaves, picking out tangles
of vines and strange, spiky plants.

Tom brushed a sticky hanging vine

out of his face. It was pale and fleshy and smelled unpleasant, and there were many more of them, dangling from the trees like grasping fingers.

"This place has an evil feel to it," he muttered.

"I haven't heard a single bird singing," said Elenna. "Why aren't there any animals in the trees?"

Maybe something has frightened them off, thought Tom.

It wasn't long before the hanging creepers and low branches forced them to dismount. Tom took out his sword and hacked through a tangle of vines and slimy ferns. The gloomy jungle was getting ever hotter and more humid, and he had to pause often to wipe sweat from his eyes.

"I can hardly catch my breath," gasped Elenna.

Tom noticed how every step took them deeper into darkness. He looked up, panting in the damp air. The branches covered the sky completely here, but as the hidden sun rose, the damp sweltering heat grew more and more intense. The sweat made his clothes stick to his body.

Cutting his way through a dense knot of vines, Tom stepped into soft green moss. It rose to his ankles, giving out a nauseating stink. He peered around.

"The ground is very wet here," he said. "The moss stretches out a long way on both sides, but I can see firmer ground ahead. We should try to cross it." Testing the squishy ground at each step, he moved forwards again.

Elenna and the animals followed, but they were only halfway across when the moss began to bubble and heave, giving off green gas that almost choked them.

Storm let out a whinny of alarm as he sank into the mire.

"Quickly!" shouted Tom, realising his mistake and lunging back through the sucking bog. "We have to pull him clear!"

Elenna and Tom snatched hold of Storm's reins and heaved with all their strength as the frightened horse struggled to get free. Even Silver caught a dangling piece of Storm's harness between his teeth, his paws sinking in the green slime as he tugged at the leather strap.

They finally managed to haul Storm to firmer ground.

"If this carries on, we'll be too worn out to fight," said Elenna, her expression grim.

Tom nodded. He looked around, feeling a strange prickly sensation between his shoulder blades. "I think we're being watched," he said.

"By a Beast?" asked Elenna.

Tom touched the red jewel in his belt, using its power to try and seek out the presence of a Beast. "I can't sense one nearby," he said.

Silver trotted forward and disappeared into the undergrowth, scouting ahead as he often did. He let out a sudden yelp.

"Silver!" yelled Elenna, putting an arrow to her bow as she leaped over gnarled roots to find him. Drawing his sword, Tom followed.

They found the wolf rolling on the ground, snapping at a thick plant tendril that had wrapped itself around his belly. The tendril was dragging him towards a huge yellow flower head that hung near the ground. The thick petals gaped like a hungry mouth. Tom spotted a scattering of small bones around the great fleshy stem.

"It's a meat-eater!" Tom shouted. "Kill it – quickly!"

Elenna shot an arrow into the flower head. It twitched and writhed, thrashing on the ground.

Tom flung himself forwards, using both hands to bring his blade down on the tendril, cutting it in two. Thick yellow slime spurted out as the tendril snaked back into the flower head.

"There are more," Tom cried as a host of the hideous flowers began to open around them. "Get out of here!"

Elenna dragged the tendril from around Silver and they ran for safety.

"We must keep close together from now on," gasped Tom.

He heaved a branch aside and saw a

wide pool of water, its clear surface rippling from the bubbles that rose from its depths.

"I think this is a natural spring," Tom said, as they gathered at the edge. "It should be safe to drink."

Silver and Storm began lapping at the shining water. Tom kneeled and scooped some into his cupped palm while Elenna filled her flask.

Trailing weeds waved gently under the surface of the water. Tom saw something glinting beneath them. He leaned further out.

"There's something metal at the bottom," he said. "It looks like…a compass." He peered more closely through the quivering water, spotting larger pieces of metal. "I see a breastplate as well, and an armoured glove." The weeds moved aside and Tom found himself gazing down at a collection of thin white objects.

He sprang up. "There's a skeleton down there," he cried. "Get back! The pool is dangerous."

"Surely not," said Elenna, her hand in the water. "It tastes so sweet."

Tom reached out to pull her away, but before he could catch hold, something tugged at her from under the surface.

Elenna let out a sudden scream of terror as she overbalanced and fell headlong into the seething water.

3

STRANGLEWEED

"Elenna!" Tom cried. His friend's legs thrashed as they were pulled under. Tom could see weeds tangled tightly around her arms.

The weeds are alive – and they're pulling Elenna to her death.

Tom flung himself onto his front, plunging his hands into the pool. He snatched hold of Elenna's ankles but she slipped from his grasp.

She struggled under the water, reaching up for Tom's hands. He saw fear twisting her face as more weeds wrapped themselves around her chest and neck.

Silver howled as his mistress was swallowed by the pool. Storm neighed and stamped his hooves in alarm at the water's edge.

Tom immediately sprang up, drawing his sword and diving headlong into the foaming water.

Swimming down, he hacked at the weed that had looped itself around Elenna's neck. It came loose and floated away, but another arm of weed groped up from the depths, its fronded end closing over her face like a green hand.

As Tom drew back his arm to strike again, a weed snagged his wrist. Bubbles of shock poured from his open mouth.

They're so strong!

He struggled to free his arm, but the tendril tightened its grip. He could feel his hand becoming numb. He writhed in the water as more weeds glided around his chest, squeezing his ribs, and then his throat.

Tom stared down in horror – Elenna's eyes were bulging with panic and her mouth opened to let out a rush of bubbles.

We're both going to drown! I can't believe it's going to end like this, after everything we've been through.

From the corner of his eye, Tom

saw a shape dart down into the
water. It was a girl, swimming
strongly towards him, holding
something that looked like an axe.
As the girl came closer, Tom saw even
more weeds streaking up from the
bottom of the pool in her direction.

He stared into the girl's eyes,
pointing towards Elenna with his

free hand: *Save her first!*

Moving as nimbly as a fish, the girl swam past Tom and Elenna, diving down to the very bottom of the pool.

What is she doing? Isn't she going to help us?

A moment later, Tom felt the weed fronds' grip loosen around his body. He swam over to Elenna.

They locked hands and he turned,
clawing at the water with his free
hand, kicking hard with his legs as
he towed her upwards.

Tom felt Silver's teeth close around

his collar as he broke the surface of the pool. The wolf heaved, helping to haul Tom and Elenna up onto dry land. They lay side by side, coughing and spluttering. *A moment longer under the water and it would have been too late.*

Tom sat up, gulping in air. The strange girl appeared, bursting up through the water and clambering quickly out of the pool, dragging some of the weed with her. Water ran from her long dark hair as she leaned over them. She wore a patchwork of tanned skins shaped into a tunic.

"Thank you for saving us," Tom said to her.

"You're welcome," replied the girl.

"I'm Imma. You must be strangers around here to let yourself get caught by strangleweed." She held up the clump of twitching weed. "You have to cut it at the root."

Tom got to his feet, helping Elenna up. "We're Tom and Elenna," he said. "We've come from King Hugo's palace. The king will reward you with gold when he knows how you helped us."

The girl frowned and shook her head. "I don't want gold," she replied. "If you wish to repay me, then help me find my brother, Polk."

Tom hesitated. He felt bad. He would have liked to help the girl, but they couldn't turn away from their Quest.

Imma eyed him closely. "Polk was taken by a monster," she pleaded. "Please help me."

Tom shared a quick glance with Elenna. "What kind of monster took him?" he asked.

"It was like a gigantic monkey," Imma said, with a shudder.

Tikron, Tom thought. *So the Beast is close.* He looked grimly at Imma. "Take us to the place where you last saw Polk," he said. "We know about the Beast, and I'll make you this vow – while there's blood in my veins, I will do all that I can to bring your brother back to you alive."

THE VILLAGE IN THE TREES

Tom and his companions followed
Imma as she made her way on bare
feet through the jungle.

"There are no paths," he said to her.
"How do you know your way?"

She looked at him with amusement
over her shoulder. "I've lived here
all my life," she replied. "The jungle
can be dangerous, but every member

of my tribe knows how to travel through it."

Thank goodness we met her, thought Tom. *I have no idea how we would have survived otherwise.*

Imma guided them through the tangles of branches. Although the route she followed was narrow, even Storm was able to pick his way through without too much trouble.

Suddenly she halted.

"What's wrong?" asked Elenna, her hand straying to her bow.

"It's a trap set by my people," said Imma, pointing to the jungle floor. Tom noticed that a coil of a creeper lay on the ground, wound into a loop and tied. Imma gestured to a heavy branch that hung suspended above them. "If you had tripped it, that branch would have swung down and crushed your skull."

"Your people don't like visitors," said Elenna, staring up at the dangling branch.

"We don't trust outsiders," admitted Imma.

"And I thought the jungle was deadly enough already, what with all the with meat-eating plants and strangleweed," said Tom.

"And now there's a Beast as well," said Elenna.

Tom nodded. "Can you tell us anything else about the creature that took your brother?" he asked Imma. "Did it have any black markings?"

The two corrupted Beasts that they

had already encountered had each been cured of Kensa's spell when Tom cut away a part of their body that had turned black. Tom hoped Tikron might be defeated in the same way.

"I don't remember," said Imma. "I only saw it for a moment. It had teeth like long, jagged knives and horrible, evil eyes."

A series of sharp clicks and whistles came down from the trees. Imma stood still, staring upwards. Tom gripped his sword, ready to fight if enemies had come upon them.

But Imma responded by making more clicking and whistling sounds.

Silver growled warily, the hackles rising all along his back. Storm whinnied, his eyes rolling, his hooves pawing the ground.

A rope ladder suddenly snaked down from the canopy of branches above them. "Welcome to my village," Imma said.

She began to climb. As she came to the dense roof of leaves and branches, a whole section of the jungle canopy slid silently aside. Tom saw faces peering watchfully down at them. He also noticed the glint of weapons.

"Aren't you coming up?" Imma asked. "You'll be quite safe with me."

"We can't leave our animals alone in the jungle," Tom said.

"You won't have to," said Imma. "Wait there." She disappeared into

the hole and, a few seconds later, a
second gap appeared. A wicker basket
about the size of a small hut was
lowered to the ground on thick ropes.

Storm eyed the basket suspiciously,
but Tom took his reins and led him

inside through an open panel. Silver
followed Elenna. They secured the
panel and the basket was winched
slowly upwards.

Tom felt a little alarmed. The
wicker carrier creaked and groaned,
the large basket swaying on the end
of the straining ropes. It seemed that
at any moment something would
break and they'd be sent plunging
back down to the ground.

But they came up safely through
the hole. Tom gazed around himself
in amazement. Scores of treehouses
nestled in the branches, some no
more than huts, but others were as
large as grand halls, built around
tree trunks and supported on great
spreading branches.

It's a whole village, he thought, *hidden away up in the trees!*

A network of walkways and suspended bridges wound through the village. Folk dressed in simple skins and furs came and went. Tom noticed that none of them were wearing shoes as they moved sure-footedly among the high branches.

Imma led Tom and his companions along a walkway to one of the largest of the treehouses. The villagers watched them with a mixture of surprise and suspicion, but no one tried to stop them.

They passed through a high, carved doorway and found themselves in a large chamber lined with tiers of seats. Most of the seats were filled with elderly men and women in dark green robes. They all stared at the newcomers.

A harsh voice croaked. "How dare you bring strangers to our village?"

"Elders of the tribe," called Imma. "I found these people and their animals in peril in our jungle. I do not believe they mean us any harm."

"That's the truth," said Tom, stepping forward. "We are warriors, battling Evil in this land. We will help you to find Imma's brother."

A burly man with long hair stepped out of the shadows. "This is no warrior," he spat. "He's a ground-crawler spy, sent to trick us."

"You're wrong, Wick," said Imma. The man she had addressed

pointed to Tom and Elenna. "He will bring other ground-crawlers," he said. "They will cut down our trees and burn us out!" He pulled a stone dagger from his belt, pointing it at Tom. "I demand the right of trial by combat. If I win, the strangers shall be put to death. If I lose, they must vow to depart and speak to no one of this place."

"We have come here in peace," insisted Tom, holding his hands up. "I will not fight you."

"I will!" said Elenna, stepping in front of Tom. "And if I win, you must allow us to stay in the jungle and fulfil our Quest!"

"No!" cried Tom.

Wick eyed Elenna, sneeringly.

"So be it!" called one of the elders before Tom had time to pull Elenna back. "Let combat begin!"

With a wild roar, Wick flung himself at Elenna, his arm raised, the deadly blade jutting from his fist.

KNIFE AND BOW

Elenna sprang aside and the warrior's swipe went wide. He staggered forwards and fell to his knees, cursing loudly. Elenna slid her bow off her shoulder and held it out in both hands, like a fighting-staff.

Elenna never uses her arrows on a human if she can avoid it, Tom thought. Wick looked fierce and powerful, but Tom knew Elenna had formidable fighting skills of her own.

Wick got to his feet, turning with a scowl. He strode towards Elenna, slicing with the knife, forcing her backwards. Silver growled, but Tom held his hand out to the wolf.

"Stay back," he said. "This has to be a fair fight."

The wolf's eyes shone dangerously, but he obeyed Tom's words.

Wick loomed over Elenna, trying to grasp her bow with one hand while he stabbed at her. Elenna ducked beneath his swipe, and brought one end of the bow up into the man's stomach.

Wick doubled up with a grunt. Elenna leaped up over his bowed head, somersaulting in midair and landing sure-footedly behind him. She swung her bow and the end struck a hard blow across the warrior's backside.

"Well done, Elenna!" shouted Tom.

Wick's face was red with rage as he turned and flung himself at her again. Elenna danced aside to avoid the knife-thrust and brought the bow cracking down on Wick's scarred, hairy knuckles.

With a roar of agony, Wick lost his grip on the knife and it clattered to the floor. Elenna twisted on her heels and jabbed the bow into the back of Wick's knees.

His legs knocked from under him, the warrior crashed to the ground.

Elenna was on him instantly, her feet on either side of his chest, an arrow on the string of her bow, the point aimed at his heart.

"Yield!" she panted.

"Never!" gasped Wick.

One of the elders got to his feet, his hand raised. "The contest is ended," he called. "The ground-crawler has triumphed. They have earned the freedom of the jungle. Concede defeat, Wick."

Wick's lips twitched for a moment and his eyes blazed. But finally he spoke. "I concede."

Elenna stepped away from him and Wick got to his feet, his face twisted with hatred.

Silver trotted over to Elenna's side, rubbing up against her. Storm stamped a hoof and whinnied.

"Can we begin to search for Polk now?" asked Imma.

"You may," said the elder. "But it will not be an easy task. We have searched for a whole day and night and have found no trace of him."

"The boy is dead for sure," said Wick, with a sneer.

"No!" cried Imma. "I'd know if he'd been killed."

"We'll find him," Tom told her. "Trust us."

"You do not know the jungle," said the elder. "Wick shall be your guide."

Tom glanced warily over at the glowering warrior. *Tracking down a Beast and fighting it in this deadly jungle will be hard enough,* he thought. *Can we trust Wick not to try and get his own back on us?*

But Tom knew they couldn't afford to waste time arguing with the elders of the jungle tribe, and so he nodded in agreement.

"May good fortune attend your hunt," said the elder. "Go now."

Imma came to Tom's side as he strode from the hall. "We should split up," she said. "Wick and I can travel through the trees, while you and your animals follow us at ground level."

"Good plan," Tom agreed.

A short while later, Tom and his companions were back on the jungle floor, following Wick and Imma as they swung and leaped through the trees. Tom saw that Imma's axe was tucked into her belt.

He marvelled at the ease with which the two jungle-dwellers travelled among the branches. They hardly rustled the leaves and vines as they speeded along, lithe and sure-footed.

"This was where Polk went missing," Imma called down after a while.

Tom pointed up to where the

branches were torn and broken. "Something big came this way for sure," he said to Elenna.

"Tikron?" she asked, peering upwards through the canopy of leaves.

"I think so," said Tom.

Silver let out a growl and went gliding through the undergrowth.

"He's found a scent," said Elenna.

Tom followed the wolf through the thick vines and creepers.

He heard shouting from above.

"Be careful!" cried Imma.

As Tom pushed onwards, a shadow moved through the branches ahead of him. He narrowed his eyes, trying to make sense of the massive form. Was it Tikron?

A terrible screech filled his head

and he flung his hands over his ears
– but it could not stop the deafening
noise drilling into his mind, sapping
all the strength from his limbs,
making him feel sick and dizzy.

As he stumbled, a huge, midnight-
black shape came swinging down
through the leaves.

Snake! Tom thought as the
creature scythed towards him.

It slammed into his chest, lifting
him off his feet and sending him
crashing helplessly to the ground.

6

EASY PREY

Tom scrambled to his feet, his chest burning from the blow. He drew his sword, his head still spinning from the ear-splitting screech that rang down from the branches.

He stared upwards. *Where's the snake gone?*

Elenna sprang through the undergrowth, arrow to her bow, aiming upwards to where the branches rocked and shook.

The black thing swung again. *It's not a snake but a tail,* Tom realised. *A long, hairy tail!*

"It's Tikron!" Tom cried.

The Beast squatted among the branches, great gnarled claws clutching the tree limbs above him. His hideous, snarling face glared down, lips drawn back from jagged fangs. As Tom watched, Tikron launched himself from the tree.

"He's coming!" shouted Tom, but his warning came too late. The monkey-Beast dropped. Elenna lifted her bow to protect herself, but Tikron's swinging arm smashed it in two and sent her spinning to the ground with a cry of anguish.

The size of the enraged and corrupted Beast horrified Tom. Kensa's spell had warped and twisted Tikron's mind, making his eyes glow yellow with evil madness.

I have to aim for the tail, thought Tom. *It's always the blackened part that contains the worst of Kensa's Evil infection.*

The Beast bounded towards Tom, hands grasping, fangs champing. Spittle sprayed through the air on wafts of disgusting breath. Tikron rammed his fist forward, but Tom flung himself behind a tree to avoid the blow.

Tikron's tail came whipping around the tree and Tom leaped high to avoid being struck. The Beast swung around the tree and kicked out.

Tom lifted his shield. It absorbed the worst of the blow, but pain still seared through his arm and shoulder. He backed away, weaving from side to side as the furious monkey-Beast pressed home his attack.

Tom dodged a flying punch and jumped high as the raking tail swept through the undergrowth. He struck at the Beast with his sword, but Tikron was horribly quick. He swung up into the trees to avoid Tom's blows.

Tikron sprang from one tree to another, his thick tail lashing dangerously. Tom flung himself to the ground as the tail grazed over his back. He was on his feet again in an instant, but Tikron attacked again,

smashing branches and ripping up
creepers. He hurled them at Tom,
yellow eyes burning.

"Tom!" It was Imma's voice, high in
the branches. "Lure him this way!"

He saw the girl scurrying from tree
to tree above.

I hope she's got a good plan!

He ran back through the undergrowth to find Storm. Silver was standing over Elenna. "I'm only winded," she gasped. "Just give me a moment."

"Come when you can," said Tom, leaping into Storm's saddle and urging the animal on. He kept his head down to avoid being thrown from the horse by low branches. Tikron roared as he caught sight of the galloping horse. Tom tugged at the reins, making Storm veer from side to side to avoid being struck as he crashed headlong through the jungle towards Imma.

Over his shoulder, Tom saw Tikron ripping branches down and

shouldering smaller trees aside as he raced to catch the fleeing horse. Just ahead of Tom, Imma swung through the trees.

"Where are we going?" Tom called up to her, hearing the roars behind grow louder.

Tikron was gaining ground.

"Make your horse jump when I say!" shouted Imma. "Trust me!"

What choice do I have?

"Now!" shrieked Imma. Tom gathered the reins and squeezed with his knees. Storm reared up in a long jump. Branches whipped Tom's face as they soared through the air.

They landed with a thump.

Tom heard a sudden whiplash sound, followed by creaking and

cracking. Looking over his shoulder, Tom saw Tikron being lifted up into the air with a loop of creeper tight around his ankle.

Imma lured him into a trap!

Tom reined Storm to a halt. He jumped down and walked back to where the Beast hung suspended upside down. Tikron was roaring furiously, his claws snatching at the air and his free leg kicking uselessly.

Elenna came running up with Silver at her heels.

She stood next to Tom, staring up at the captured Beast.

"Is it over?" she gasped. "That seemed too easy."

"I just have to cut off his tail, and Kensa's spell should be broken," Tom

said, watching the long black tail as it whipped to and fro above his head.

Wick came leaping down from the trees, brandishing his spear. "It was a trap set by my people that caught the demon," he cried. "It's for me to slay it!"

"No!" shouted Tom, stepping forward. "We don't kill Good Beasts. They can't help themselves."

"I won't listen to you, ground-crawler," snarled Wick. "If you get between me and my prey, I will slay you as well."

"Don't, Wick," called Imma, sliding down a creeper to the jungle floor. "We need the monster alive to show us where Polk is."

"Foolish child," said Wick. "Your brother is dead. I shall slay this demon and wear his pelt for a cloak! I will be the greatest warrior our people have ever known."

He drew back his arm, the point of

his spear aimed at the Beast's heart.

"Stop!" Tom shouted, bounding forwards and knocking the warrior off balance. Wick's spear scythed through the air, missing the Beast's chest, but gouging a bloody gash across his side. Hissing in agony, Tikron thrashed wildly as his blood sprayed down.

"Fool!" raged Wick, drawing his dagger. "You are both in league with this demon!"

"No!" shouted Elenna, staring upwards in horror. "Look!"

The creeper holding Tikron was fraying under his weight. With a twang it snapped and Tikron plunged to the ground. He scrambled to his feet, his mouth wide as he let out a deafening shriek. Tom and the others staggered and fell, throwing their hands over their ears.

Tom couldn't think, he couldn't fight – all he could do was try to crawl away and hide from the Beast's terrible noise.

Still screeching, Tikron ran off through the trees, one arm pressed against his bleeding side. As the dreadful noise lessened, Tom got to his feet again.

Thanks to Wick's meddling, the Beast had escaped.

A sudden blow from behind flung Tom onto his face. He turned over, gasping in pain. Wick was standing over him, his face contorted in rage, his dagger aimed at Tom's neck.

"We should never have trusted an outsider," he snarled. "You helped the demon escape. Now you will pay with your life!"

He lifted the dagger high and brought it down with a swift and deadly blow.

1

7

THE SILENT JUNGLE

Tom grasped Wick's wrist, struggling against the warrior's strength, the dagger close to his throat. Gradually, the man's weight and power forced Tom's hands back. Tom flinched as the sharp blade nicked his skin. The jungle-dweller was too big for him to throw off.

"Stop!" Imma's voice rang out. She ran up to Wick and punched the side of his head. "Leave him alone!"

Releasing Tom, Wick drew back, rubbing his ear.

"You would side with a treacherous ground-crawler?" snarled Wick.

"He has promised to help find Polk," Imma said. "While there's a chance my brother is alive, I won't let you harm him."

Tom got to his feet. Elenna stood nearby, watching Wick cautiously.

The big warrior thrust his knife into his belt. "Polk is dead," he said. "When we return to the village, the elders will hear of your betrayal." He turned. "The demon is injured – tracking him will be simple now. And this time he will not escape my vengeance." He leaped away through the trees.

Elenna stooped and picked up the spear that Wick had used to wound the Beast. She peered at the ground. "There are drops of blood here," she said. "Wick is right about one thing: we should be able to follow Tikron without too much trouble."

"But a wounded Beast may be even more dangerous," Tom warned.

They headed into the trees. Tikron had left a trail of destruction in his wake: smaller trees had been ripped from the ground, and the undergrowth was trampled. All along the route, the leaves and ferns were spattered with blood.

Tom took the lead, Elenna just behind. He could see Wick up ahead now, the knife in his fist again.

Imma walked at Tom's side. "You

haven't told us the real reason why you came here," she said. "You know all about this monster. How could that be? And you didn't want Wick to kill it. Is Wick right – are you in league with the creature?"

"No," Tom said firmly. "Not at all. Tikron has something that I need. If he is killed, I may never find it. And there's something else. Tikron is not a monster. He's under an Evil spell, and I may be able to cure him." He looked at her. "I'm sorry I didn't tell you the truth before."

Imma shrugged. "I trust you."

"But what are we to do when we catch up with the Beast?" asked Elenna. "When he screeches, I can't think straight. I can barely stand.

How can we fight against something like that?"

"I've been wondering that myself," Tom replied. "What we need is something to plug our ears so we can't hear it."

Imma glanced at him. "We could use strangleweed," she said. "My people dive for fish in the jungle pools, but many of the pools are infested with creatures we call brainworms. They burrow into your ears and lay their eggs inside your head. To stop them, we put strangleweed in our ears."

Tom stared at her. It was a strange idea, but it might work. "Are there any pools nearby?" he asked.

"Wait here," said Imma. She

ducked off to the side. A few moments later she returned carrying a writhing mass of strangleweed in her hands. She showed them how to wrap the quivering weed around their heads, so that the thin tendrils could slide into their ears.

Tom found the sensation unpleasant, but he was surprised by the sudden silence that came when the weeds had clogged his ears. He shuddered as he felt the tendrils moving slowly in his ears.

This is really risky, he thought. *I can't hear a thing. What if Tikron circles around and comes at us from behind?*

But Silver and Storm would still be able to hear. If Tikron tried to

ambush them, Tom knew his animal
friends would make the sort of fuss
that he could see.

Imma took the lead again, and they
pushed on through the jungle. The
brief pause meant that Wick was
now out of sight, but Tikron's trail

of devastation and spilled blood was easy to track.

They came to a clearing. At its centre stood a huge rotten tree, bare of leaves and with its mighty twisted branches reaching up like broken fingers into the sky. Wick stood beneath it, staring silently upwards.

There was something in the crook of the tree. A small boy, trussed up in vines. His head was free and his eyes were open as he shouted something to Imma, who was running towards him. Then, apparently weakened, his head nodded and his eyes closed.

As Tom stepped into the clearing, he saw a massive form spring from the outer trees, darkening the sky as it leaped for the broken branches and landed in the rotten tree, towering over the trapped boy, glaring down at them with eyes filled with loathing.

Tikron has come to guard his prey!

1

FISTS OF FURY

Tom gripped his sword and lifted his shield as he stared up at the terrible Beast. There was dried blood in the matted fur on Tikron's side, but the wound seemed to have closed. Kensa's spell was protecting the Beast even as it turned him Evil.

Tom saw Silver and Storm rearing up, striking the air with their claws and hooves.

Tikron's jaws gaped and he let out a
shriek that Tom only heard as a faint
hissing. The strangleweed had made
Tikron's most deadly weapon useless.
But Wick crumpled to his knees,
covering his ears.

Tom strode forward, his sword raised. Elenna was at his side, holding the spear in both hands.

The Beast stared down at them, sudden bewilderment in his eyes.

Although his ears were plugged, the power of the red jewel in his belt gave Tom the ability to hear Tikron's voice in his mind.

Why do you not fall to your knees at the sound of my voice?

The Beast widened his jaws and shrieked again. In obvious pain, Wick rolled on the ground, his hands clamped to the sides of his head.

"No slave of Kensa's will ever defeat me!" shouted Tom, brandishing his sword. "Come down, Tikron, and face me in battle."

Shaking with rage, Tikron snapped off a long branch and flung it down. Tom brought his sword around in a scything arc. The blade cut the branch in two, and the broken pieces crashed harmlessly to the ground.

Tom turned to Imma, then pointed to Polk: *Go and get your brother.*

Imma raced for the tree. Her nimble fingers dug into the rotting bark and she climbed quickly.

Stinking foam sprayed from Tikron's open mouth. He stamped his feet and shook the branches in his fury. He fixed his bloodshot gaze on Tom and leaped down from the tree into the clearing.

Tom charged. As Tikron raised his fists to crush him, he dived forwards, rolling between the Beast's legs. He jumped up and spun around, raising his sword to cut off Tikron's blackened tail.

But the jungle master was not so easily fooled. He jerked his tail away and Tom's sword dug deep into the trunk of the tree, the impact sending

a jolt of pain through his shoulders.

Tikron's voice blazed loudly through Tom's head.

Did you think it would be so easy? You will not defeat me as you have defeated so many before. I will tear you limb from limb and scatter your broken body through the jungle as a warning to others!

Tikron's fist came down like a mallet. Tom bounded aside, glancing up to see that Imma had almost reached her brother.

A few moments more and they will all be safe!

He couldn't see Wick. Had the warrior fled in terror?

Tom saw Elenna waving her arms wildly, her mouth moving in

desperate shouts that he couldn't hear. She looked like she was trying to warn him of something…

Tom spun around, seeing Tikron's tail lashing towards him at ground level. He tried to jump, but he was too late. His legs were knocked from under him and he crashed heavily to the ground.

Tikron towered over him, claws balled into hideous fists. Tom huddled under his shield as powerful blows rained down on him, the hammering fists shaking him to the bone.

He saw Elenna racing in from the side. Gripping the spear in both hands, she rammed the butt end into Tikron's injured ribs.

Even with his ears plugged, Tom

heard the Beast's roar of agony.

Tikron turned on Elenna, his face
a mask of rage, his massive fingers
spread to snatch at her. She danced
back, thrusting and striking at the
Beast's hands with her spear.

"You'll never catch me, Tikron!"

she shouted, her words only just audible to Tom – the strangleweed was beginning to weaken. "Surrender to us, and save yourself."

She leaped, twisting in midair and using the spear to help her vault into the lower branches of the rotten tree.

The Beast bellowed, lunging up and grasping at her ankles. Elenna jumped high, stabbing down at the claws. She climbed on as Tikron jumped up to catch her.

Tom could see Imma, high in the tree, racing along a level branch, her trussed-up brother slung over her shoulders. They came to the end of the branch and Tom realised that she was preparing to make the jump to the nearest tree. It was a long way, and with Polk's weight to bear, Tom could understand why Imma hesitated.

Elenna climbed higher, but Tikron stopped, his head turning as he caught sight of Imma. He let out a roar and shook the trunk of the tree.

Tom heard the Beast's voice sounding in his head.

My prey! It will not escape!

Tikron swung towards Imma. As the Beast approached the two small figures, Tom watched in helpless horror as Imma screamed, almost dropping her brother.

Tikron's hideous face showed no mercy as he slowly extended a long, sharp claw.

He's going to kill them both!

9

MAYHEM IN THE TREES

Tom saw the blood drain from Imma's face as the Beast climbed up towards her. Her shoulders were bowed under Polk's weight and sweat was running down her face as she tried to reach the higher branches.

Tikron clawed his way up, drawing closer and closer.

Desperate for an idea, Tom saw a

coil of dead vine hanging from the rotten tree. *Will it bear my weight?*

He had to risk it – Tikron had almost reached Imma. Sheathing his sword and securing his shield on his back, Tom ran for the vine. He leaped high, catching it between his hands.

It creaked, but it held his weight as he began to climb hand over hand up into the tree.

"Tikron!" he shouted. "Why bother with such small prey when you can have me?"

Tikron paused, glaring down at him. But then his lips curled in a sneer.

I will slaughter you later, little warrior, said the menacing voice in Tom's head. The Beast began to climb again.

Imma had almost reached the end of the branch she was standing on. She was moving more slowly now, testing the thinning branch before putting her weight on it. There was a look of pure terror on her face.

She knows she's trapped. Tikron will catch her.

Tom set his jaw. "Not if I can help it!" he said aloud, even though he could barely hear his own voice.

He jumped from the vine and landed on a branch near the trunk. Here the branches were thick and straight and he could clamber up them far more swiftly.

If I can just get above Tikron, I might be able to stop him.

The Beast was moving more slowly now as he came to the outer branches – they were barely big enough for him.

Tom glanced down. Storm and Silver were visible far below, but he couldn't see Elenna anywhere. He teetered on a branch, swinging his arms for balance, clutching at the flaking bark on the trunk.

Not so sure of yourself up in a tree, are you? Tikron's mocking voice came into his head.

Tom managed to regain his balance in time to see the Beast clambering down towards him.

At least I've saved Imma for the time being, he told himself.

But how well could he battle the Beast up here? Tikron was in his element, and it was all Tom could do not to slip and fall. He pulled his shield around onto his arm and drew his sword. He stepped cautiously along the branch to meet the Beast. He wobbled, spreading his arms for balance.

Tikron's eyes glinted with evil pleasure. He landed on Tom's branch, gripping it with his feet. He flung his weight from side to side to make the branch sway.

Tom crouched low, one hand on the branch to steady himself. He watched the Beast carefully, waiting for his next move.

Tikron jumped high and came down on the branch again with his full weight. It dipped terrifyingly. Tom was thrown forwards, snatching at empty space. He tumbled – *smack!* – into another branch. The fingers of his left hand managed to grab hold as his legs dangled over empty space below, but his shield went spinning away to the ground. His sword was

still in his other hand – but his grip
was loosening on the branch.

*What do I do? Should I drop my
sword to help myself hold on? No!
I can't face Tikron without a weapon.
He's too dangerous.*

Tikron came stalking along the

branch. His lips were drawn back from his fangs in a grin of wicked triumph. The Beast stood over Tom, staring down at him with a mocking look in his yellow eyes.

Tom's shoulder burned with agony as he clung on. His fingers were numb from the effort of gripping the branch. If he fell now, his blood would stain the ground and his Quest would have failed.

No! Never!

Tikron lifted one huge foot and slowly brought it down onto Tom's hand. Tom gritted his teeth as he felt his bones grinding.

Behind Tikron's hate-filled stare, he could almost see Kensa's dark eyes, filled with glee as she watched.

Tom reached up with his sword, but Tikron ripped down a branch and used it to swipe the blade to one side.

Tom winced in agony as the dreadful weight of the Beast pressed down even harder. *There's only one hope – and that's for us both to fall. Even if I die, Tikron may be dazed enough for Elenna to defeat him!* Tom stared down, his heart hammering. *I have no choice!*

He lifted his sword again, hacking at the branch. His first blow cut a deep white gash in the rotten wood. He drew back his sword-arm and cut again. The branch began to split.

The voice echoed in Tom's head. *No!*

The branch gave way.

Tom fell, branches and twigs

slapping and whipping him as he plunged downwards. Tikron was also falling, his weight snapping off branches one by one.

Tom reached out blindly, feeling coarse fur under his fingers. He had caught hold of the thick hair around Tikron's ankle.

He came to a sudden, jarring stop, his legs swinging as he clung grimly to the Beast's fur. His head swam as he tried to make sense of what had happened. The ground was still far below. Above him, Tikron was dangling precariously, his face twisting in pain. The Beast had managed to loop his tail around a thicker branch, and his arms and legs were groping frantically for some other hold. The strangleweed in Tom's ears had frayed enough that he could hear quite clearly how the branch creaked dangerously.

Tom saw a movement to his left. Elenna was picking her way cautiously along the branch, the spear in one hand. That's why he hadn't seen her on the ground earlier – she'd been climbing the tree.

Tom stared up into Tikron's eyes. They burned amber as a hideous grin curled the Beast's lips.

Tikron's voice edged into Tom's mind. *You are doomed!* The Beast reached down and began to prise Tom's fingers loose from his ankle.

Tikron was going to make Tom fall – he was going to watch him die.

10

THE LASH OF EVIL

As the Beast wrenched Tom's fingers from his ankle, his yellow eyes widened in shock. Suddenly, the two of them were plunging headlong down through the branches again.

Tom spun over as he fell, arms up to protect his face. He waited for a shuddering impact with the ground, and certain death.

He came to a sudden stop, the

breath knocked out of him. He had landed on his back, on something soft and warm. He opened his eyes and found himself staring up into Tikron's face.

The Beast's eyes had returned to their original warm brown, and had lost every trace of Evil.

"What...?" Tom managed.

Then he realised he was lying in Tikron's cradling palm.

He caught me!

Tom heard the jungle master's voice in his mind. *I am so sorry, Master of the Beasts – I could not fight the power of the sorceress's spell.* Tikron set Tom down, hanging his head as if in shame.

Tom was still trying to understand

how Tikron's change had happened.

He glanced up and the truth hit him in an instant. High in the tree he could see Tikron's blackened tail, still looped around the branch. And close by he saw Elenna's spear, jutting from the wood. She had thrown the spear and severed the Beast's tail. The spell was broken. Tikron was himself again.

Elenna jumped down from the lower branches and ran to Tom's side.

"You took quite a risk up there," Tom told her.

"What other choice did I have?" she replied. She looked anxiously at the Beast. "Is he cured?"

At that moment, Silver and Storm came racing up. The wolf sniffed Tikron then nudged the Beast with his forehead, whining softly.

Tikron reached out gently to ruffle Silver's fur.

"They remember one another from the Quest in Rion," said Tom, smiling.

Storm walked over to a bush at the edge of the clearing. He struck the ground with his hoof and looked back at Tom. The terrified faces of Imma and Polk stared through the leaves. Imma had managed to carry her brother out of the tree and had cut away the vines which bound him.

"You're safe now," called Tom. "The Beast is Good again."

Imma and Polk emerged cautiously, staring at Tikron, but quickly became bolder when they saw that he meant them no harm.

"You must come back to our village," said Imma. "The elders will wish to honour you."

"We can't leave here yet," Tom said. "Tikron was sent here to guard a magical ingredient I need – the red root of the hidden tree." He stared around. "But I don't know where to look for it."

Tikron let out a grunt. He shambled to the foot of the rotten tree's great trunk. He drew back his arm, then smashed his clawed fist through the crumbling bark, ripping out chunks of wood.

Tom ran to his side and saw that the Beast had revealed the tree's hollowed-out heart.

Tikron stood aside and Tom leaned into the wound. Deep within the tree, a slender pale sapling was growing, weak and frail and no taller than the length of Tom's hand.

Tikron's long arm reached past

Tom and gently pulled the sapling
up, root and all. Tom saw that it had
red roots.

"Thank you, Tikron," said Tom, as
the Beast laid the plant in his hands.

The very moment Tikron released
the plant, he vanished from sight.

"Where ever has he gone?" Polk

gasped, his eyes round with wonder.

"The Good Beast has gone to protect another kingdom," said Elenna, with a smile. "Now we can return to your village and tell them the good news."

The Council Hall in the trees buzzed with excitement as Tom and Elenna finished telling the village elders of their adventures.

"Our people owe you a great debt of gratitude," said one of the elders, smiling widely. "If there is anything we can do in return, you have only to ask. You must certainly attend the Feast of the Full Moon – it is only two days away."

Tom shook his head regretfully. "Thank you, but I'm afraid that won't be possible," he said. "We must continue our Quest."

"Not so fast!" said a rough voice behind them. They turned to see Wick stride into the hall, a bow in his hands.

"I have never trusted ground-crawlers," he said. "I have always believed they mean us harm."

Tom was about to draw his sword to defend himself and Elenna when a wide smile broke out on Wick's face. "You have taught me better," he said, holding the bow out to Elenna. "This bow has been in my family for ten generations," he told her. "Yours was broken – I want you to have this."

"Thank you very much," Elenna said, taking the bow. "I'll treasure it, in remembrance of your people."

"Now we must be gone," Tom said.

The elders rose and cheered as Tom and Elenna made their way out of the hall and down the rope ladder to where Silver and Storm were waiting patiently.

They mounted Storm, waving a final farewell to Polk and Imma as they headed off.

Tom noticed that this part of the jungle seemed less gloomy. Shafts of sunlight falling through the trees lit their path. But he knew they could not let their guard down.

"There's still one Beast left," he said grimly as they rode.

Elenna nodded. "Falra the Snow Phoenix," she said.

Kensa is cunning. She'll have left the most dangerous Beast to last.

Tom had a feeling that they were about to face their deadliest foe ever.

"Where to now?" asked Elenna.

"The map will show us in good time," Tom replied. He drew his sword and raised it high. "But wherever we're sent, I'm ready to fight Kensa's wickedness."

THE END

CONGRATULATIONS, YOU HAVE COMPLETED THIS QUEST!

At the end of each chapter you were awarded a special gold coin.
The QUEST in this book was worth an amazing 11 coins.

Look at the Beast Quest totem picture on the page opposite to see how far you've come in your journey to become

MASTER OF THE BEASTS.

The more books you read, the more coins you will collect!

Do you want your own
Beast Quest Totem?
1. Cut out and collect the coin below
2. Go to the Beast Quest website
3. Download and print out your totem
4. Add your coin to the totem
www.beastquest.co.uk/totem

READ THE BOOKS, COLLECT THE COINS!
EARN COINS FOR EVERY CHAPTER YOU READ!

550+ COINS
**MASTER OF
THE BEASTS**

550+
515
480
445
410
395
380
365
350
320
290
260
230
217
206
191
180
146
112
78
44
30
19
8

410 COINS
HERO

350 COINS
WARRIOR

230 COINS
KNIGHT

180 COINS
SQUIRE

44 COINS
PAGE

8 COINS
APPRENTICE

Don't miss the next exciting Beast Quest book in this series, FALRA THE SNOW PHOENIX! Read on for a sneak peek...

CHAPTER ONE

THE FINAL BEAST

Tom slashed his blade through the snaking vines. Sweat poured off his face and his tunic stuck to his back. Imma, a girl of the tree people, had shown them the way to go. It was her way of saying thank you, after they had liberated Tikron, a giant monkey that had been terrorising the jungle.

But we're wasting time even so, Tom thought. *There's one more Quest to face and we're still struggling out of the jungle.*

Finally, he saw clear daylight ahead.

"This way!" he called to the others. "We're almost there."

Elenna led Silver and Storm through the dense foliage. Soon they reached the edge of the trees. Tom unfolded the map given to him by the wizard, Aduro. He pointed to the far north of the kingdom.

"This is where we need to go next," he said.

"The Pit of Fire," Elenna read over

his shoulder, from the map.

"It's the perfect lair for Falra the Snow Phoenix," said Tom.

Falra, who was once our friend. But now she's our enemy.

Tom folded the map and stuffed it away angrily. Kensa had stooped to new depths, turning Good Beasts to Evil. She'd cast a spell over young Beasts from Rion, those unable to protect themselves. So far he'd managed to free three of them – Tikron, Vislak and Raffkor. Only Falra remained in Kensa's thrall.

It wasn't just Falra's life at stake. Kensa had poisoned the twin dragons, Vedra and Krimon, with lunar blood. Krimon had succumbed, and his brother was stricken with the poison.

With every day that passed, Evil spread through his veins. By the next full moon, that very night, the transformation would be complete. The only way to cure him was by mixing four ingredients, each guarded by a Beast of Rion. Tom had claimed three, but Falra guarded the fourth.

And if I know Kensa, the final fight will be the most deadly.

Storm shook a vine free of his hooves and reared up.

"Someone's glad to be out of the jungle," said Elenna. She stooped to stroke Silver's back, but the wolf bared his teeth and growled. "What's got into you?" she asked.

Tom felt his skin prickle and the hairs on his neck rose. He quickly

drew his sword half out of his
scabbard, as the air seemed to wobble.
A shape was appearing…

"Daltec!" he cried with relief,
sheathing his sword.

But the young wizard's face was

unsmiling, serious.

"You must hurry!" he said, striding towards them. "Vedra becomes more and more severe. His scales…they're almost completely black now."

"We'll ride to the Pit of Fire at once," Tom said grimly.

"It's too far," said Daltec. "Even for Storm at full gallop. You'll never make it there, and then back to the palace, before nightfall."

"Can't you magic us closer to the Pit of Fire?" asked Elenna.

"Perhaps," said Daltec, "but it's a long way, and there are four of you…"

"Please try!" said Tom.

"It's dangerous," said Daltec, twisting his robes with a nervous hand. "You might come to harm if my magic isn't strong enough."

Tom glanced at Elenna. She gave him a firm nod, as though reading his thoughts. "Forget the risks," he said determinedly. "We can't let Kensa's plan succeed!"

"Very well," said Daltec. "I need you all to face north, in the direction of travel."

Tom tugged Storm's head around, and planted his feet north. Elenna stood at his side with Silver.

"Good luck," said Daltec. He raised his hands towards them, took a deep breath and closed his eyes. His lips moved in a silent spell.

Golden light sparked across the wizard's fingertips, then shot towards Tom and his companions. A white orb surrounded them. Through it, Tom saw the landscape drain of colour. A frown crossed the wizard's face, growing into a grimace of pain. The light from his hands came in waves, flashing and dying.

"He can't do it," said Elenna. "He's not strong enough!"

Daltec gritted his teeth, his whole body starting to shake. Golden sparks scattered around them.

A roar erupted from the wizard and blinding light made Tom clamp shut his eyes.

Then all went silent.

Read
FALRA THE SNOW PHOENIX
to find out more!